Mummy on the Nile

by **Susan Aguilo**

Illustrations by **Mike Motz**

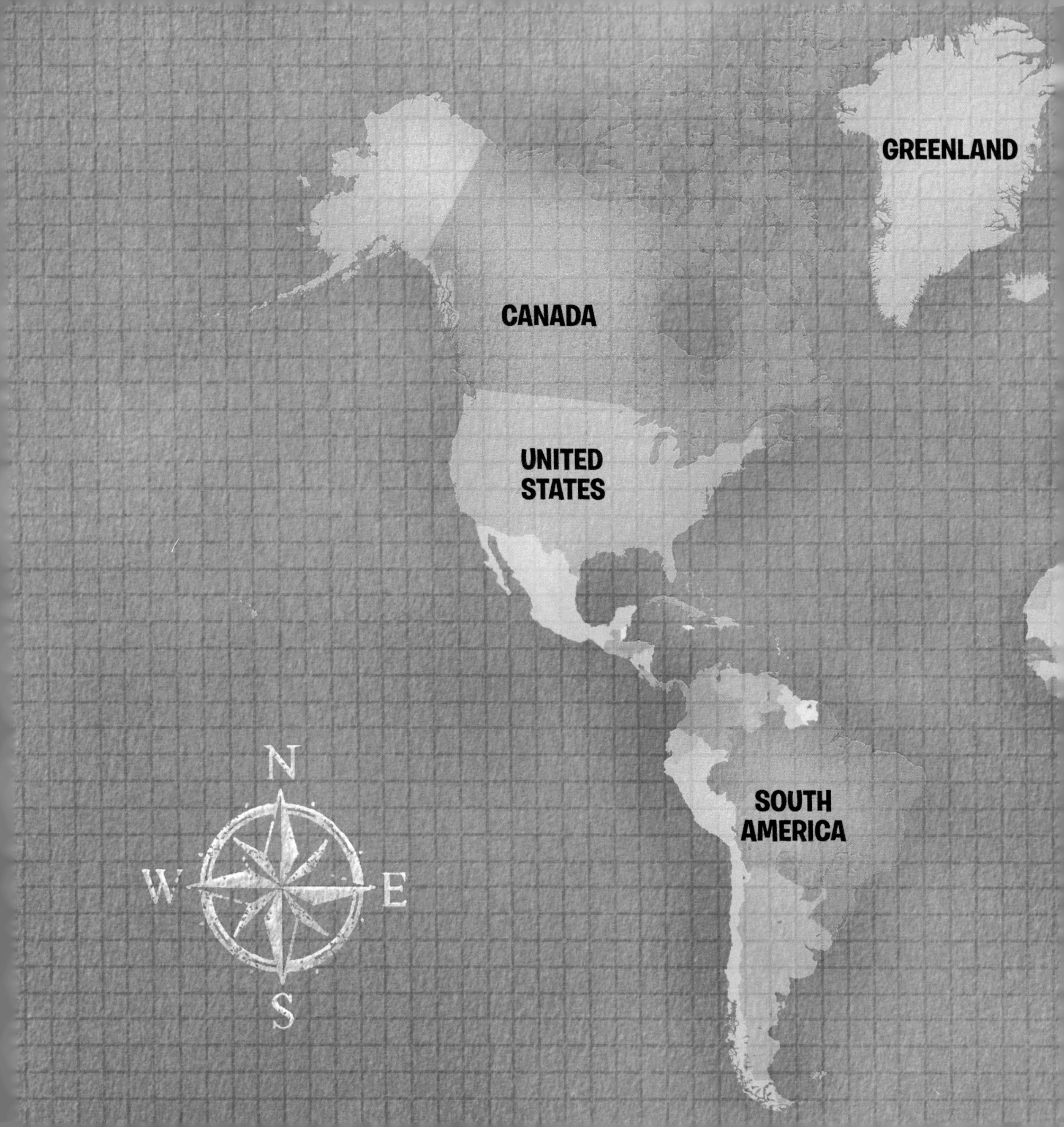
GREENLAND
CANADA
UNITED STATES
SOUTH AMERICA
N
W
E
S

ISBN-13: 978-1502364579

Alex spent the day on a class trip to the Royal Ontario Museum. They saw giant
dinosaur bones, the bat cave, giant crystals, and even a meteorite, but his favourite
was the gallery for Egypt. He thought the mummy and hieroglyphics were amazing!
They even learned how a mummy was made and how to spell their name
in hieroglyphics. He thought that was so . . . cool!

After coming inside, having his shower, and brushing his teeth, it was time for bed.
Even though he hated going to sleep, he loved this time of the day because his
mom would tell him amazing stories where he was the adventurer.

Alex's mom came in the room, lay down on the bed, and started her tale.
Tonight it was **"A Mummy on the Nile."**

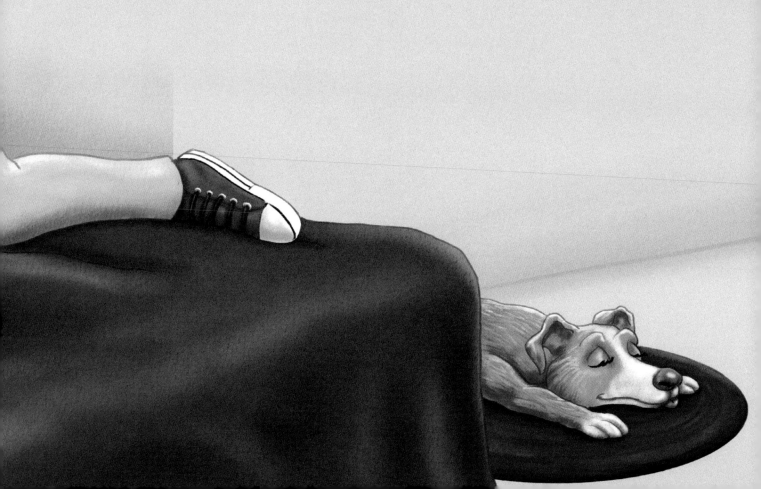

Alex, his cousin Victoria, and his best friend (and dog), Elmo, arrived in Cairo, Egypt for a vacation down the Nile River.

They rented camels to tour the pyramids and the great sphinx.
The sight was breathtaking!

As Alex helped Elmo off their camel, Victoria's camel tripped and did a face plant into the sand, throwing Victoria over its head. Picking herself up off the ground and brushing herself off, she leaned over to check her camel. Just as she leaned in, it spit. **SPLAT!** Victoria let out a disgusted noise while cleaning the front of her shirt.

Alex smirked. "WOW! How did you manage to crash a camel???"

Victoria just scowled at him!

Victoria spent the entire day taking pictures and videos of herself, Alex, and Elmo going through each of the pyramids. They climbed the tallest one just in time to watch the sunset before making the long trip back to their hotel.

The next day they toured the museum and famous bazaar. Alex bought some souvenirs, a treat for Elmo, and even some street food from the vendors.

They came upon one vendor who was selling jewelry. Victoria's eyes caught sight of a snake bracelet with big ruby eyes. After finally agreeing on a fair price, Alex, Victoria, and Elmo continued through the bazaar with Victoria beaming brightly with her new bracelet.

That evening they boarded the sleeper train where they would have dinner and sleep the night while traveling in style towards their next destination.

Alex wasn't sure what woke him, but when he heard the door he sat straight up in his bunk. His eyes were still adjusting to the darkness when he noticed someone leaning over Victoria. At that same moment Victoria woke up with a scream, and Elmo started to bark. Alex swung out of the bunk as his feet hit the man square in the head. The man stumbled back from the blow and made for the door.

When Alex got into the hallway he saw it for what it was: "**A MUMMY!!!!**" He gasped.

It turned when he spoke, and it let out a scream and jumped from the train. Alex ran to the opening, but there was no sign of it.

After encountering the mummy, both Alex and Victoria were shaken and had a hard time going back to sleep, unlike Elmo who lay on his back snoring. Alex and Victoria were both tired when the train finally came to a stop.

They found their guide at the station waiting with their dune buggies. They were staying the night in tents in the desert and would be taking dune buggies to get there. Before Victoria could even get into hers, Alex and Elmo were off like a shot. Alex loved to drive fast and went from one hill to the next at top speed. Victoria raced behind them in her buggy, laughing as they drove over hills and down valleys, spraying sand everywhere.

Like ancient travelers in the past, they took a break at the temple of Hatshepsut and toured around.

Victoria thought she saw a mummy in the shadows of a pillar, but when she showed Alex, there was nothing there. Feeling a little unsure, they decided to continue on their way to the oasis.

After another hour of travel they could see the oasis in the distance.
It was a majestic sight of sand, white tents, palm trees, and camels.

Alex placed his foot on the gas and sped towards the oasis. He had had a lot
of fun and was still smiling like crazy when he arrived. As Victoria parked,
she bumped a tree. Alex shook his head and Victoria grinned; they gave a
high five as Elmo shook the sand out of his fur.

After a short rest in their tent they came out to find the sun setting. The Bedouin people who ran the Oasis had set up dinner under the stars. The area was covered in beautiful printed carpets to keep the sand away from the food. They joined a group of travelers from Germany and England at low tables in front of one of the tents. They laughed and talked and learned about the history of the Bedouin people.

Once the food had been served, music started to play and dancers came out to entertain them with a traditional belly dance. Some of the belly dancers had snakes draped around them.

They watched the dancers as they ate. One of the belly dancers looked towards Victoria and saw the bracelet on her wrist and stopped. She looked scared, and before running away she said, "Beware! The bracelet is cursed!"

Alex and Victoria looked from the bracelet to each other in shock.

Later that night Alex woke to Victoria whispering his name. Alex lifted his head in the cot beside hers and looked over at her. She was pointing to the side of the tent at a perfect silhouette of a **MUMMY!!!!**

Alex ran outside, but when he got there, he found nothing. When he went back into the tent, Victoria was holding Elmo's collar and shivering.

The following morning they travelled to the temple of Karnack, and with the help of the curator they learned about the bracelet. This led them to the pillars with the five snakes. The curator translated the hieroglyphs on the pillar.

"If the bracelet of Rah is disturbed, the mummy will wake and walk the earth until its return." Reading further they discovered the resting place was in Abu Simbel in a statue. "Only with the return of the bracelet will the mummy's curse be lifted."

Victoria, Alex, and the Curator stood, puzzled. Finally Alex shook his head and grumbled, "Someone must be playing a joke on us!"

Late that afternoon they arrived at the boat that would take them the rest of the way down the Nile River. After stowing their bags they wandered the deck, meeting some of the other passengers.

They met Krista Lina, a friendly teacher from Canada with her little dog, Rambo, who had been travelling Egypt on summer break. Rambo sat in her purse and eyed Elmo warily. They also met Deb and Barry, a funny retired couple whose children had bought them this vacation for their 25th anniversary present.

They all stood on deck, watching as the boat left the dock to slowly steer down the river. They enjoyed the cool breeze at sunset after the contrast of the sand dunes the night before.

After the last couple nights, Alex decided to set a trap for the mummy, so he went about getting everything he needed from the boat. He collected rope, an old cargo net, wooden pulley, and a hook. He rigged it to a lever and mechanical pulley system for the dinghy. When everything was in place, he sat up to watch Victoria's cabin door, with Elmo at his feet.

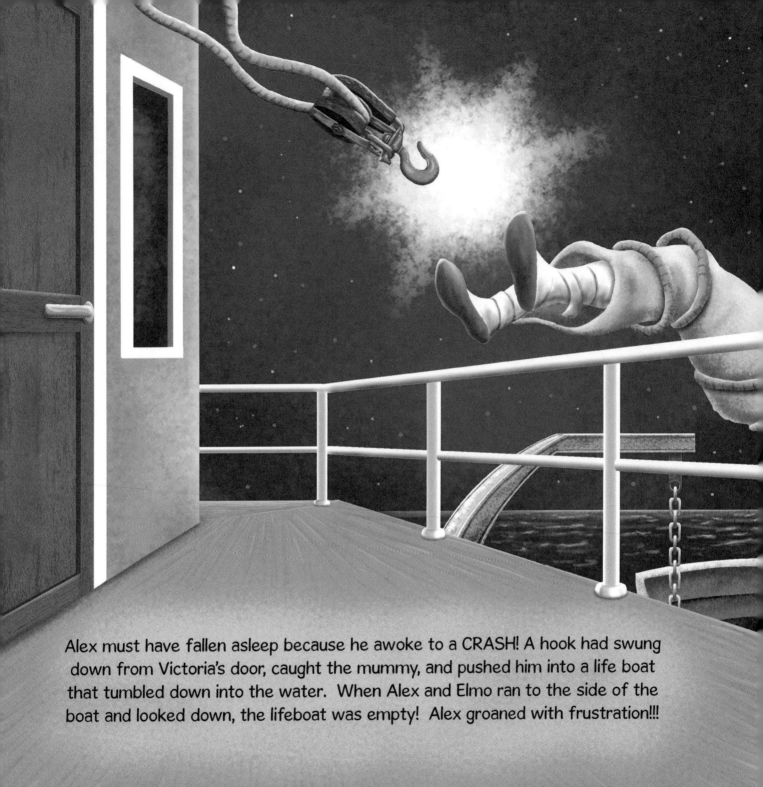

Alex must have fallen asleep because he awoke to a CRASH! A hook had swung down from Victoria's door, caught the mummy, and pushed him into a life boat that tumbled down into the water. When Alex and Elmo ran to the side of the boat and looked down, the lifeboat was empty! Alex groaned with frustration!!!

That morning they toured the ruins in Aswana, ate in an outdoor café, and even went to a bazaar.

On their way back they stopped to watch a street performance. It was a man seated on the ground; a basket lay in front of him. As he raised a flute to his lips, the music flowed enchantingly. The basket started to move until a snake head slowly rose from its depth. Elmo gave a low growl as the snake climbed higher and higher with each note, flaring its chest out, for it was a **KING COBRA!**

Suddenly the music stopped, and the snake hissed! Victoria, Alex, and Elmo
took a step back as the old man stared with wide eyes at Victoria's bracelet.
The snake charmer pointed and hissed, "That bracelet is cursed." Victoria agreed
but they had no idea how to return it. The man thought about this and remembered
that the builder of the statue liked to make hidden drawers and usually had
a disguised button or a decoration that must be twisted.

Looking up at the sky Alex snapped his fingers and turned to Victoria and said,
"I have an idea, but it is going to take some planning. Let's get back to the boat."
Running, they waved their thanks!

A couple of hours later they arrived at a balloon tour. Elmo jumped in as Victoria stowed their bags while Alex convinced the young guide to help them. As they floated up, Alex turned to Victoria and the guide and said, "Take us to Abu Simbel."

"Aye, Aye, Captain," Victoria said with a salute.

The view from the air was spectacular as they followed the Nile River at sunset. Soon they could see Abu Simbel in the distance. As they got closer Alex put a harness on and secured it to the side of the balloon. Once they reached the ruins, Victoria took the balloon down and Alex climbed over the side and slid down the rope.

Now hanging from a rope below the balloon, he reached for the statue.
A gust of wind came out of nowhere and slammed the balloon against the ruins.
WHOOOSH! The lines caught and started to rub against the stone;
the balloon began to shred and deflate.

Hanging below a deflating balloon Alex prepared to finish his task. Feeling a tug on the rope he looked down with surprise to see the mummy climbing below!

Victoria started throwing her shoes down at the Mummy hoping to slow it down.

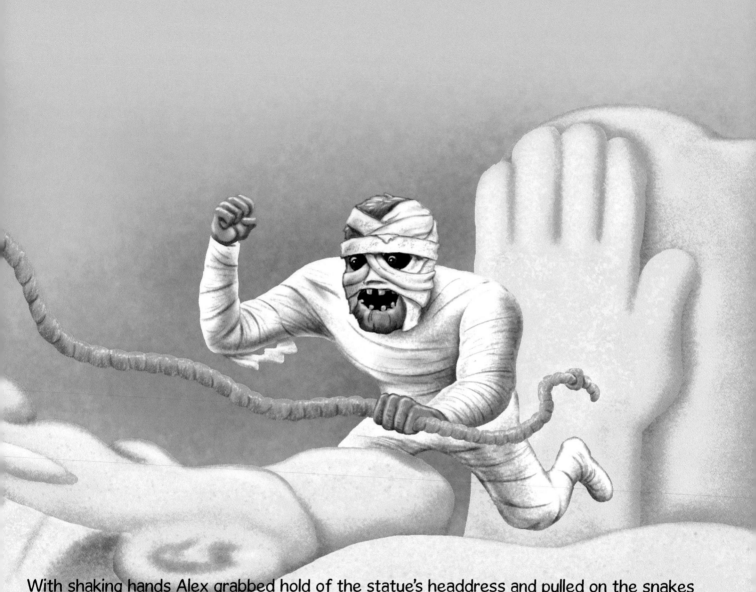

With shaking hands Alex grabbed hold of the statue's headdress and pulled on the snakes head. It popped out with an imprint of the bracelet snake charm. Alex carefully placed the charm into the slot and the snake head snapped closed.

With the return of the bracelet, Alex looked down to find the mummy waving his fist before disappearing into a cloud of dust.

Alex looked up to see Victoria, the guide, and Elmo looking down at him. Elmo was wagging his tail and barking with excitement, and Victoria was smiling and shaking her head. She shrugged and said, "I guess we won't be getting our deposit back."

So that was where Alex hung, waiting for the Egyptian police
to pull them off the side of the ruins.

He smiled, shook his head, and wondered how he was going to explain this one.

Alex's mom smiled and said **"The End."**

That was the story of **"Mummy on the Nile."** His mother leaned over, kissed Alex lightly on the cheek, and said, "Until tomorrow night, and your next adventure!" She winked and said, "Sleep tight."

The End

Did You Know? Fact or Fiction

Egypt: is one of the most populated countries in Africa and the Middle East. The majority of its over 84 million people live near the Nile River. The Sahara Desert, which covers most of Egypt's territory, is sparsely inhabited.

Primary Language: Arabic

Regional Animals: Hippos, crocodiles, jackals, scarab beetles, scorpions, cobras

Nile River: is a major north-flowing river in northeastern Africa, generally regarded as the longest river in the world. It is 6,650 km (4,130 miles) long. The Nile is the primary water resource and life artery for Egypt.

Great Pyramid of Giza: is the oldest and largest of the three pyramids. It is the oldest of the seven wonders of the Ancient World and the only one to remain largely intact.

Great Sphinx: is a limestone statue of a mythical creature with a lion's body and a human head that stands on the west bank of the Nile near the Great Pyramid of Giza. It is the largest single stone statue in the world, standing 241 ft long, 63 ft wide, and 66.34 ft high.

Temple of Hatshepsut: This temple is considered one of the great achievements in Egyptian architecture. It is similar to Greek architecture developed thousands of years later and marked a major turning point in Egyptian architecture.

Oasis: is an isolated area of vegetation in a desert, typically surrounding water. Caravans must travel via oases for trade and transportation so that supplies of water and food can be replenished.

Abu Simbel Temples: are two massive rock temples in Abu Simbel. They are situated on the western bank of Lake Nasser. They were originally carved out of the mountainside for Pharaoh Ramesses II and his Queen Nefertari. However, it was relocated in 1968, on an artificial hill. The relocation was necessary to avoid their being submerged during the creation of Lake Nasser.

DON'T MISS A SINGLE ADVENTURE

collect all of the Alexander books at
www.abedtimeadventure.com

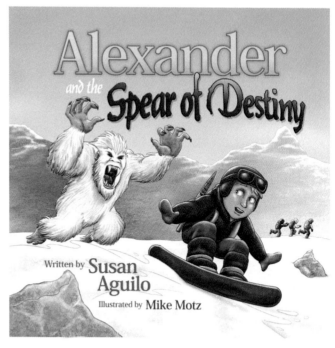

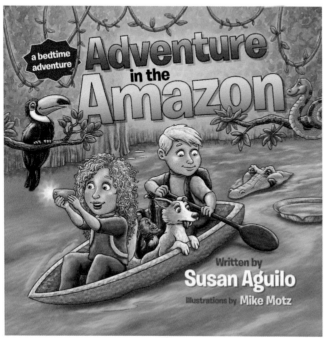

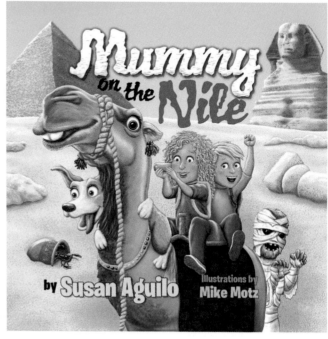

Manufactured by Amazon.ca
Bolton, ON

10372772R00026